MacGooses' Grocery

by Frank Asch · pictures by James Marshall

PARENTS' MAGAZINE BOOK CLUBS, INC.

To Robert Kraus
F. A.

For William James Gray
J. M.

The MacGooses owned a
grocery store and every day
they sat in it together
waiting for customers.

OUR TURNIPS ARE TOPS

CREAM OF JUNEBUG SOUP

SAL ON SP

OUR TOMATOES ARE GOOD ENOUGH TO EAT!

Mrs. MacGoose not only had to sit in the store, she had to sit on her new egg.

GOOD SPUDS

COME AGAIN

PIC

One day, Mrs. MacGoose got tired of sitting on her egg, so she put Mr. MacGoose in charge and went for a walk.

Soon Mr. MacGoose got tired of sitting on the egg,

so he put Junior in charge
and he went for a walk.

Soon Junior got tired,

so he put Sis in charge and he went for a walk.

Soon Sis got tired.

She put the egg in charge
and went for a walk.

With everyone gone, the baby inside the egg soon got cold.

He put on some warm clothes, but he was still cold.

Just then some playful weasels
came into the store,
and seeing no one around,
they decided to have some fun.

They built mountains with all the food

. . . and knocked them down.

When the weasels heard the MacGooses coming,
they ran out the back door, leaving
the egg near the stove.

Soon it was so hot inside the egg that the baby goose
had to take off all his clothes.

When Mrs. MacGoose got back and saw
the mess, she nearly fainted.

"It's not my fault," said Junior, "I put Sis in charge."

"It's not my fault," said Sis, "I put the egg in charge."

Just then . . .

. . . the egg hatched.

"Never mind whose fault it was," said Mother MacGoose.
"It's too nice a day to worry about that sort of thing."

"That's right," said Father.

And they all went for a walk.

THE END

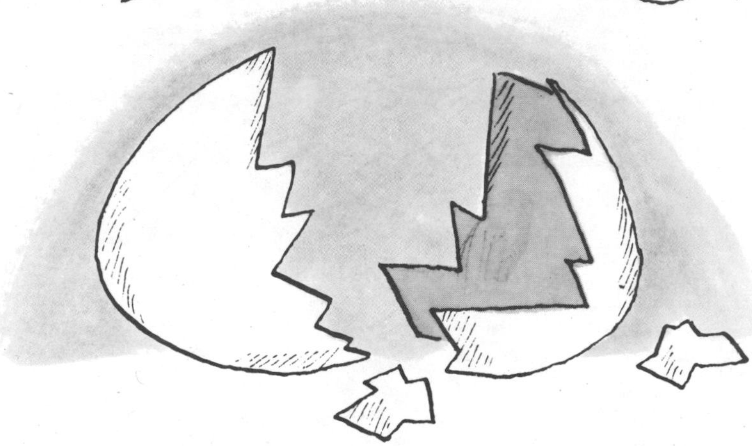